Scholastic Publications Ltd.,
10 Earlham Street, London WC2H 9RX, UK

Scholastic Inc.,
730 Broadway, New York, NY 10003, USA

Scholastic Tab Publications Ltd.,
123 Newkirk Road, Richmond Hill,
Ontario L4C 3G5, Canada

Ashton Scholastic Pty. Ltd.,
P O Box 579, Gosford, New South Wales,
Australia

Ashton Scholastic Ltd.,
165 Marua Road, Panmure, Auckland 6,
New Zealand

First published by Scholastic Publications Limited, 1989
Text copyright © John Cunliffe, 1989
Illustrations copyright © Scholastic Publications Limited and
Woodland Animations Limited, 1989

ISBN 0 590 761226

Made and printed in Belgium
Typeset in Times Roman by AKM Associates (UK) Ltd,
Ajmal House, Hayes Road, Southall, London

Postman Pat's
Christmas Surprise

Story by **John Cunliffe**   *Pictures by* **Jon Haward**
From the original Television designs by **Ivor Wood**

Hippo Books
in association with André Deutsch

It was autumn in Greendale. The leaves were turning brown and falling from the trees. There was a big parcel for Granny Dryden on Tuesday morning. It was her new catalogue from Manchester.

"That's good," she said. "I'll be able to start picking some Christmas presents. Oh dear, but everything seems to cost so much these days."

Pat looked at the catalogue with Granny Dryden, whilst they had a biscuit and a cup of tea.

On Friday, Pat called on Granny Dryden again, with the Pencaster Gazette. She had papers all over the kitchen table, and a pot of ink out, and she was sucking the end of her old ink-pen and looking very puzzled.

"Whatever are you doing?" said Pat.

"It's this Christmas competition," said Granny Dryden.

"Let's have a look," said Pat.

"It was in my catalogue," said Granny Dryden, "but it isn't easy."

"Hang on," said Pat, "I'll give you a hand if you like."

Pat took the ball-pen from behind his ear, and gave it a good suck.

"Now, then," he said, "what do you have to do? Hm, yes. Look you can put that in there . . . and . . . that's sixty-five . . . and . . . oh dear . . ."

Now Pat was stuck. It was a very hard competition. There were all kinds of things to do. There was a crossword, and a word-finder, and puzzle-pictures, and some number-puzzles. Then you had to finish some sentences about things in the catalogue.

"We'll never finish it," said Granny Dryden.

"You never know what we can do," said Pat, "with a little help from our friends."

"There are some good prizes," said Granny Dryden. "You can pick anything you like from the catalogue. First Prize, items up to £2,000, and £2,000 in cash!"

"Good gracious!" said Pat. "I've never seen so much money all at once. We'll have to give it a try."

"There's a spare copy of the questions," said Granny Dryden. "You can borrow them if you like."

"Thanks," said Pat.

When Pat called at Greendale Farm, he showed the puzzle-picture to Katy and Tom.

"Can you name these pop-stars?" he said.

"Easy," said Katy.

"Simple," said Tom.

And they named them all before Pat had finished his glass of milk.

When Pat called on the Reverend Timms, he said, "Now, Reverend, you're good at numbers. Would you just have a look at this puzzle? I'm a bit stuck with it."

"The good Lord will guide us," said the Reverend Timms.

"Now where did I put that calculator?"

And he had the answer before Pat had finished his cup of coffee.

15

When Pat called on Miss Hubbard, he said, "Could I have a look in that big dictionary of yours, please? There's a word I'm trying to find."

Miss Hubbard pulled the huge book from the shelf and opened it on the parlour table. She helped Pat with the word-finder, and they had finished it by the time Pat had finished his glass of rhubarb-wine.

By the end of the next week, they had answers to all the questions, and Granny Dryden filled in the form in good time.

"I'll pop it in the post for you," said Pat. "And keep your fingers crossed."

The weeks went by. It became colder in Greendale. There was snow on the tops of the hills.

"It'll soon be Christmas," said Pat.

One Saturday morning, Pat called at Greendale Farm, and the twins were busy writing their letters to Father Christmas.

"What do you want for Christmas, Pat?" said Tom.

"Oh, hmmm . . . let's see," said Pat. "I'd love a really good pair of binoculars, to do a spot of bird-watching. But there's not much chance of that."

"You'd better write to Father Christmas," said Katy.

"I will," said Pat. "And what are you asking Father Christmas for?"

"A radio-controlled car," said Katy.

"A sledge," said Tom.

"There's not much chance of that," said Mrs Pottage. "But you can ask."

Pat called on the Reverend Timms. He said, "What would you like for Christmas, Reverend?"

"Well," said the Reverend Timms, "I would like a new television set. But there's not much chance of that."

"You'd better write to Father Christmas," said Pat.

"I will," said the Reverend Timms.

Pat called on Dorothy Thompson. He said, "What would you like for Christmas, Dorothy?"

"Well, I'd love a good warm pair of slippers," said Dorothy. "But there's not much chance of that."

"You'd better write to Father Christmas," said Pat.

"I will," said Dorothy. "And I'll ask for a pair for Alf whilst I'm at it. He gets such cold feet."

Pat called on Granny Dryden. He said "What would you like for Christmas?"

"Oh, there's a lovely warm coat in the catalogue," said Granny Dryden. "It would be just the thing to keep me warm in church. But there's not much chance o that."

"You'd better write to Father Christmas," said Pat.

"I will," said Granny Dryden.

Pat called on Ted Glen. He said,
"What would you like for Christmas,
Ted?"

"I need a new power-drill," said Ted.
"This one's just about worn out. But
there's not much chance of that."

"You'd better write to Father
Christmas," said Pat.

"I will," said Ted.

Pat called on George Lancaster. He said, "What would you like for Christmas, George?"

"I wouldn't mind a pair of skis," said George. "Just think how I could whizz round to feed the sheep in winter! But there's not much chance of that."

"You'd better write to Father Christmas," said Pat.

"I'll give it a try," said George.

Pat called on Miss Hubbard. He said,
"What would you like for Christmas,
Miss Hubbard?"

"A new bike," said Miss Hubbard.
"But there's not much chance of that."

"You'd better write to Father
Christmas," said Pat.

"I will," said Miss Hubbard.

The next time Pat called on Granny Dryden he had a good look at her catalogue.

"They're all in your catalogue," said Pat.

"All what?" said Granny Dryden.

"All the things our friends would like for Christmas," said Pat.

"Let me guess," said Granny Dryden, and she picked a present for each one. She got most of them right first time.

"But there's not much chance of them getting what they want," she said. "Everything costs such a lot these days."

"You never know your luck," said Pat.

They had forgotten all about the competition, it was such a long time ago that they had done it. Until, one Thursday morning quite near to Christmas, there was a special-looking envelope in the post for Granny Dryden. It was made of very thick paper and it had a gold seal on the back. When Pat brought it, Granny Dryden was busy making a cake, so she said, "Pop it on th mantelpiece, Pat. I'll open it later."

"Oh, but it looks important," said Pat. "Wouldn't you like to open it now?"

He just couldn't wait to see what was in it. But Granny Dryden only said, "Oh, no, I can't be bothered with it. I must get this cake in the oven."

So Pat didn't find out what was in it; not, anyway, until Friday morning. When Pat opened the garden gate, Granny Dryden's door flew open, and she ran down the garden path to meet him. Then she put her arms round Pat and gave him a big hug and a loud kiss. What a surprise Pat had! Granny Dryden had never done such a thing before. He said, "Oh . . . Granny Dryden . . . goodness me . . . well . . . I . . . oh . . . whatever . . .?"

"Oh, Pat, we've won!" sang Granny Dryden joyously. "We've won! We've won!"

"What . . .?" said Pat.

"The competition! We've won the competition! First prize! Come and have a cup of tea, and I'll tell you all about it."

"Competition? What? Oh? Oh, you mean . . .?" said Pat.

"Yes," said Granny Dryden. "The one we did together. It was that special letter. I popped it behind the clock and forgot all about it, being busy with that cake. Then I saw it this morning, when I was dusting. I opened it just before you came."

"Well I never," said Pat. "How much have you won?"

33

"It's how much have *we* won," said Granny Dryden. "I haven't forgotten how much you helped, Pat."

"Oh, I didn't do so much," said Pat.

"I could never have done it without you," said Granny Dryden.

"But the Reverend helped with the number-puzzles," said Pat. "And then Miss Hubbard helped with the word-finder, and the twins named the pop-stars. And . . ."

"There'll be a share for everyone," said Granny Dryden.

"There's plenty and some to spare, because we've won the first prize. What do you think of that? Remember? £2,000 in cash and £2,000 in things from the catalogue. Oh, Pat, I've had such an idea. We can make all our friends' Christmas wishes come true. We can pick their presents from the catalogue."

Whilst they drank their cups of tea, Pat and Granny Dryden went through the catalogue and picked presents for every one of their friends in Greendale.

"You'll have a busy day when all this arrives," said Granny Dryden.

"I will and all," said Pat.

"And we'll share the money," said Granny Dryden. "And there'll be some for the Church Fund, and the Save The Children Fund, and some to put by for a rainy day."

"Great!" said Pat.

It was a good thing that the parcels
didn't all arrive on the same day. There
would never have been enough room in
Pat's van, and where would Granny
Dryden have put them all? It was a good
thing that Pat had a big cellar where he
could lock all the parcels up, and keep
them as a surprise until Christmas came.

Christmas came at last. There was a
party for all their friends in the big barn
at Greendale Farm. Everyone would be
there. Sam Waldron was very puzzled
when Pat asked to borrow his van just for
an hour or two. He had never asked for it
before. In the middle of the party, Pat
arrived, flung open the door, and
shouted, "Special delivery everyone!"

39

And there was Sam's van, full of the most exciting-looking parcels, each one with someone's name on it. There was a parcel for every single person, and a lucky-dip barrel for the children.

Oh, what a time they had, opening their parcels! They had never known such a Christmas. George and Tom went out into the snow, to try their sledge and skis. Pat spotted a hawk through his binoculars. Granny Dryden was lovely and warm in her new coat. Katy's model-car was whizzing about under the tables of food. Ted helped the Reverend to fix up his new television set. Miss Hubbard had a ride round the duck pond on her new bike. And Alf and Dorothy were cosy in their new slippers.

When they had all had their Christmas
dinner, the Reverend Timms stood up
and lifted up his glass of Miss Hubbard's
best rhubarb wine, and said, "Let's drink
a toast. Let's say a big 'Thank you' to
Granny Dryden and Pat for this
wonderful party and for all their
marvellous presents. And we should say
'Thank you' to Saint Nicholas as well."

"He means Father Christmas,"
whispered Mrs Pottage in the twins' ears.

"Oh, but everyone helped with the answers," said Granny Dryden.

"Yes," said the Reverend Timms. "But it was dear old Father Christmas who put the true spirit of Christmas in the hearts of our dear friends, so that they shared their good fortune in the competition with us all. So here's to Father Christmas, and to Granny Dryden and Pat, and all the people who helped them."

Everyone drank, waved their glasses, and cheered.

43

On Saturday, Pat and Sara took Julian to see Father Christmas arriving in Pencaster. He came in a fine coach pulled by two white horses. He switched on the lights on the Christmas-tree in the market-place. Then Julian went to see him in the Town Hall. Father Christmas gave Julian a new kite, and Julian thanked him for that and for all the lovely presents he had sent for the people of Greendale.

"This is one Christmas we'll remember for a long time," said Pat.

And they did.